It's been 400 years since Shakespeare wrote his last play, yet his stories and characters are as alive today as they were when he first penned them. Students across the world study Shakespeare's plays in school, and they have been translated and performed in almost every language. So, what is it about Shakespeare's work that keeps it relevant through time? Shakespeare's language is rich, his characters are complex and dynamic, and his themes—love, betrayal, honor, bravery, war, politics—are still relevant today.

In this Play On Shakespeare series, we take a lighthearted approach to these classic stories in the hopes of introducing Shakespeare's timeless characters and themes to a new generation of readers.

How to enjoy this book...

Shakespeare's works are not only famous for how entertaining they are and the lessons they teach, but also they are filled with important literary devices. Pay attention to the color of the words as you read along to see what literary device is being used!

GREEN words show SETTING—where the story is taking place.

PURPLE words show the CHARACTERS—who is in the story.

YELLOW words show FORESHADOWING—hints about what is going to come next.

PINK words show SIMILES—comparisons that use the words "like" or "as."

ORANGE words show ALLITERATION—two or more words that start with the same sound.

BLUE words show IMAGERY—descriptive words that can be experienced by one of the five senses.

Also note that Shakespeare's plays are separated into "acts," which are the sections of a play, just like chapters are sections of a book. Pay attention to something that happens in each act, and see if you can remember something from each act at the end! For more ideas on how to enjoy this book, please visit FlowerpotPress.com.

Designed by Flowerpot Press
in Franklin, TN.
www.FlowerpotPress.com
Designer: Stephanie Meyers
Editor: Johannah Gilman Paiva
DJS-0912-0136
ISBN: 978-1-4867-0855-0
Made in China/Fabriqué en Chine

A **Play On** William Shakespeare's

A MidSUMMeR NiGHT'S DReaM

Adapted by
Luke Daniel Paiva

Illustrated by
Roberto Irace

Hermia–
A passionate young Grecian maiden* who is in love with Lysander, even though her father has betrothed her to Demetrius. ("Betrothed" means to promise to marry someone.)

* Grecian maiden means a girl from Greece.

Helena–
A determined young Grecian maiden* (see note to left) who is friends with Hermia, and in love with Demetrius, even though he does not love her in return.

THE COURSE OF TRUE LOVE

Setting: The Fairy Wood, hidden deep in the forest near Athens, Greece.

Fairies–
The community of magical creatures who live in The Fairy Wood.

Spoiler alert: The play "A Midsummer Night's Dream" is known as one of William Shakespeare's comedies, which rather than meaning the play is funny, means that though there may be some trouble during the story, it has a happy ending.

Lysander–
A kind young Grecian gentleman* (see note to left, but substitute "guy" for "girl") who is in love with Hermia, though her dad, the nobleman Egeus, disapproves.

Demetrius–
A confident young Grecian man (there is no explanation needed, I hope) who is in love with and betrothed to Hermia, though she does not love him in return.

NEVER DID RUN SMOOTH

Puck–
The most mischievous fairy, also known as Robin Goodfellow.

King Oberon—
The King of the Fairies, who is sometimes mischievous, and a little vengeful, but still believes in love.

Queen Titania–
The Queen of the Fairies, who is irritated with her husband's antics, firm in her beliefs, and still believes in love.

Nick Bottom–
The town weaver. and amateur actor, who thinks very highly of himself, and as a result, is often the butt of jokes.

And so Act I ends and our story truly begins...

Act II

Deep in the woods of Greece, there is a clearing where you will find the greenest grass, the tallest trees, and the most colorful flowers—most of which you have never seen before in all your life.

These woods have had many names throughout the centuries, but none truer than "The Fairy Wood."

Fairies are notoriously mischievous, and though they mean no real harm, they do like to play tricks on humans who travel through their woods.

Just ask our four lovesick wanderers, Hermia, Helena, Demetrius, and Lysander, about the night they ran away, through The Fairy Wood, in hopes of overcoming their star-crossed* love.

Hermia ran away with her true love, Lysander, so her father could not force her to marry Demetrius.

Demetrius ran into the woods after Hermia, in hopes of still marrying her.

Helena ran after Demetrius, who she desperately loves, though he does not love her in return.

Love is very complicated sometimes.

*A love that is prevented from happening by an outside source. (Another way of saying bad luck in love.) Back then, people thought the stars brought about these kinds of troubles.

Shortly before dusk, after ages of meandering through the thickest forest they had ever seen, and arguing about who should rightfully be married to whom, the lovesick wanderers tumbled down a small hill, and landed in an opening at the heart of The Fairy Wood.

They were no worse for wear and mesmerized by the beauty of the wood. However, they were not alone. The air was filled with magic, and they grew drowsier with every step. When they could resist the magic no more, they laid down to rest in the midst of the meadow.

Just beyond the meadow, on the outskirts of the forest, two bluer than blue eyes twinkled with delight. Those eyes belonged to Puck, who watched Hermia, Helena, Demetrius, and Lysander drift off to sleep.

Though his parents had named him Robin Goodfellow, he was known throughout the realm as "Puck."

Puck's hair was as wild as a holly bush and as black as night. His eyes were ice blue and shone brightly, even in the dark. And he had a scruffy, hairy chest like a billy goat.

If you were to see him, at first you would want to laugh out loud, but you would quickly swallow your chuckle and flee for fear of his mischievous retribution.

On this particular evening, Puck had already been delighting in magical mayhem, and it had given The Fairy King Oberon an idea. Puck had stumbled across Nick Bottom, (who often acted even more foolishly than his name sounded), rehearsing a play in the woods with his friends. Puck overheard the boastful babbling of Bottom and decided it would be amusing to give him the head of a donkey.

At the same time, Oberon was having a bit of an argument with his wife, the Fairy Queen Titania, and decided to use Puck's help to play a little joke.

As Puck entertained King Oberon with his tale of transformation, the King thought of another use for Puck's powers. He ordered Puck to race around the globe and fetch a magical flower with powers of persuasion beyond compare.

Puck was instructed to orchestrate a meeting between the donkey-headed actor Bottom, and a magically bewildered Queen Titania (courtesy of the flower). The Queen would fall hopelessly in love with Bottom, and the King would have his laughs at her expense.

You might be thinking that magically making your queen fall in love with an actor who has the head of a donkey is a bad idea. You're right; it's a terrible idea, but sometimes people make bad choices when they're upset.

Fortunately, King Oberon and Puck didn't always meddle meanly. King Oberon had also overheard our four Grecian wanderers arguing on their journey through the woods. Not wanting to see one more heartbroken relationship, Oberon ordered Puck to use the special flower and his powers of mischief to make the star-crossed lovers see the foolishness of their arguing.

Puck descended into the meadow and danced from flower patch to flower patch, plucking petals and humming a sweet melody that seemed to drift across the entire meadow.

By the time he finished preparing for his joke, the four humans had fallen fast asleep.

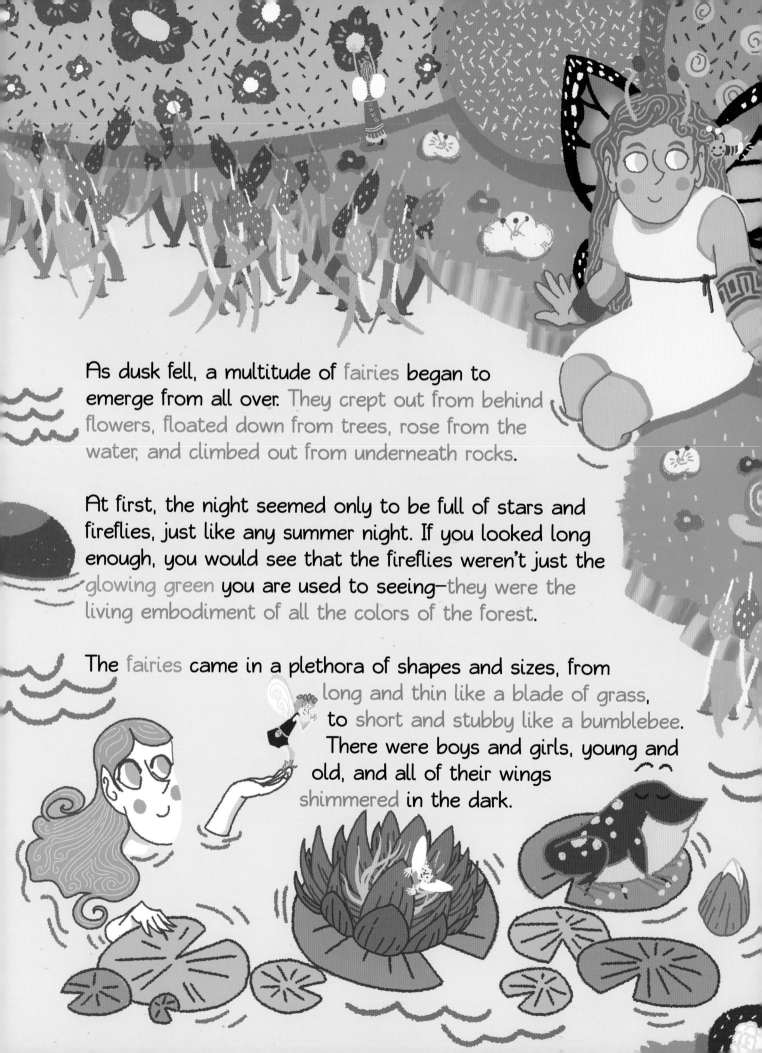

As dusk fell, a multitude of fairies began to emerge from all over. They crept out from behind flowers, floated down from trees, rose from the water, and climbed out from underneath rocks.

At first, the night seemed only to be full of stars and fireflies, just like any summer night. If you looked long enough, you would see that the fireflies weren't just the glowing green you are used to seeing—they were the living embodiment of all the colors of the forest.

The fairies came in a plethora of shapes and sizes, from long and thin like a blade of grass, to short and stubby like a bumblebee. There were boys and girls, young and old, and all of their wings shimmered in the dark.

Puck tiptoed into the middle of the now sleeping
Helena, Hermia, Lysander, and Demetrius.
He extracted the nectar from the magical flower,
and jumped onto Lysander.

He poured a drop on each of Lysander's eyes
and then fluttered to Demetrius,
doing the same.

As he sprinkled the magic
nectar, Puck whispered to the
sleepers:

"Upon your eyes
I empty all the power
of this magic flower.

When I leave, awake and rise.
See your true love
with brand new eyes."

He then retrieved his flute and looped and swirled his way around the meadow, playing a wild and beautiful tune.

"These humans came to our woods full of heartache and arguments," shouted Puck from high above all the other fairies, "let us see if we can show them a fairy good time and change the way they're thinking!"

"Hurrah!" shouted all the other fairies in response, as they raised their glasses full of dew and nectar.

PEASEBLOSSOM

MOTH

MUSTARDSEED

"My flute charms them, and I have given a special potion to the two known as Lysander and Demetrius. They will wake with new eyes.

Lysander will still love Hermia, but no longer hate Demetrius. Demetrius will see the virtue in Helena, and no longer pursue Hermia. However, it is not so easy to uncross the stars in matters of love."

COBWEB

Act III

"Our good King Oberon would like to see merriment and love instead of argument. What say you my good fairy folk? Can we help these humans see the error of their ways?" asked Puck.

Puck flew higher and played his flute louder, and with more merriment than before.

The fairies looked on, amused by the chaos of the star-crossed lovers and their antics as they tried to win each other over in the most ridiculous ways.

Love and a little magic can make you do some pretty silly things!

Meanwhile, Queen Titania was still smitten with Bottom and was having her maiden fairies wait on him hand and foot. (Perhaps King Oberon's joke had gone a little too far.)

Act IV

As the sun began to rise, and the moon began to fall, the fairies decided there had been enough fun and frolics for the night.

The four lovers were wet, and muddy, and tired, and looking ridiculous after their night of magical mayhem.

It was time to send the humans back to their homes.

Puck used a potion given to him by King Oberon
and removed the spell from Lysander's eyes.
He instructed all of them to return home and
marry the one with whom they should truly be.

WHAT FOOLS THESE MORTALS BE!

Even King Oberon managed to make up with the Queen. He hadn't yet told her that it was his idea to have her put under a spell, but he would get around to it eventually...

Puck returned Nick Bottom to his human form. The wild night of magic had inspired Bottom. As he ran back to the city to put the finishing touches on the play he had been rehearsing, he mused about the tales of his adventures and how famous they would make him.

Act V

The two couples returned to their city. They walked hand in hand and discussed wedding plans. Watching them go, Puck whispered after them that if he offended them in any way, to pardon him, and to think that they had but slumbered here while these visions did appear, and remember this night as nothing more than A MiDSUMMeR NiGHT'S DReaM.

The famous William Shakespeare was born hundreds of years ago, in 1564. He lived in the small market town of Stratford-upon-Avon with his parents, John and Mary, and seven siblings.

Kingdome of Scotland

Dublin

Ireland

Kingdome of England

Stratford-upon-Avon

London

William Shakespeare

At only 18 years old, Shakespeare married Anne Hathaway. They had three children.

Shakespeare was a busy man! He worked as an actor, poet, businessman, and playwright during the reign of Queen Elizabeth I of England, a time which became known as the Golden Age of England.

During his life, Shakespeare wrote 38 plays and 154 sonnets and came up with almost 3,000 words that were added to the English language! He even invented some of the words we use today, like "bubble" and "silliness!"

During Shakespeare's life, it was believed that fairies held a festival on Midsummer Night (June 24). To have a midsummer night dream literally means to dream about fairies!

At the time Shakespeare was alive, it was illegal for girls to act on stage, so all of the female roles were played by boys!

The Globe Theatre is famous for being the place where many of Shakespeare's plays were performed.

To my wife, for always being there.
—L.P.